Frontispiece

"TWO LONG, GRAY-VIOLET EYES THAT LOOKED
THROUGH HIS OWN, BEYOND, TO FRANCE "

HER FIANCÉ

FOUR STORIES OF COLLEGE LIFE

By

JOSEPHINE DODGE (DASKAM) BACON

WITH ILLUSTRATIONS BY

ELIZABETH SHIPPEN GREEN

Short Story Index Reprint Series

BOOKS FOR LIBRARIES PRESS
FREEPORT, NEW YORK

First Published 1904
Reprinted 1970

STANDARD BOOK NUMBER:
8369-3476-8

LIBRARY OF CONGRESS CATALOG CARD NUMBER:
73-121520

PRINTED IN THE UNITED STATES OF AMERICA

CONTENTS

ILLUSTRATIONS

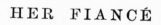

HER FIANCÉ

HER FIANCÉ

W ON'T you take him, Biscuits?"
urged Evelyn, pathetically,
"ah, do!"

Biscuits grinned cheerfully.

"Thanks, no!" she said, "I have a
Burke paper—"

A derisive shout interrupted this emi-
nently academic confession; if all Biscuits' Burke papers had been handed in,
the entire rhetoric department would
long since have been buried beneath
them, for she wrote them all the year
round, it would seem, quite regardless of
scheduled changes of subject.

"Oh, yes! I know all about that!" persisted Evelyn, scornfully. "You had a Burke paper when I wanted you to show my uncle the art gallery and the plant house. And when Tommy Sears came up unexpectedly and I had two men up for the rally, you had a Burke paper then. And you may remember that the night of the concert you couldn't sit and talk to Patsy's man while she was singing, because you had to plan out a Burke paper. Now don't be a pig, Biscuits, but take him! You're the only one in the crowd that hasn't got a man already, and it's so beastly hard to run a new program so late in the day! You can sit 'em out, if you want, but do take him!"

"My dear child, I'm sorry she's sick, but I tell you that I wouldn't take the Prince of Wales!"

"Not the Prince of Wales? Not Allbert Eddard? *Fi donc!*"

A sleepy, drawling voice issued from
under a great down puff on the couch,
and as the group of girls started nervously and stared at the tumbled pillows,
a small, sleek, silvery brown head
emerged from beneath them, and two
long-lashed violet eyes gleamed strangely
from a dark-skinned little face.

"Why, Suzanne! Have you been here
since morning? I thought you'd gone!"

"*Mais non!* I've been asleep. If it
was about me, dears, never mind—I was
fast asleep."

"Do you mean that you've slept here
since nine? It's three now," said Biscuits incredulously.

"*Tant mieux!*" Suzanne returned
lightly, "there's so much more time
gone! It's very diverting—to sleep. It

knits up the raveled sleeve of care, you know. I wish it would knit up the raveled sleeve of my organdy—the blue one. I caught it on the door-knob. *Mais, n'importe.* Allbert Eddard—*que veut-il?*"

"Biscuits wouldn't take him to the Prom," said Evelyn gloomily.

"*Mon Dieu! Et pourquoi pas?* I would. 'Allbert Eddard,' I'd say, 'though your mamma oppresses the Irish and though your conduct has often left much to be desired, nevertheless, if you've brought your evening clothes, I'll take you, *mon cher!*' "

"You might take this one, then," suggested Evelyn, morosely. "He's got the same name."

"The same name?" queried Suzanne. She was stretching herself awake like a cat, yawning and swaying slenderly from side to side.

HER FIANCÉ

"Albert G. Edwards, Yale, '9—,"
Evelyn responded briefly; "maybe it's
he, anyhow?"

"*C'est bien possible,*" agreed Suzanne.
"In disguise. *Quelle veine!* And the G.
is for Guelph! Now wasn't that foxy of
him? Am I to take him, really?"

Evelyn stared incredulously.

"Oh, Suzanne, would you? Could you?
It would be so sweet of you! He's Emily
Thayer's *fiancé* and he's never been up
before, and she's got the grippe and she
can't see him at all, and I promised her
I'd look out for him, and at the last minute my second and third men telegraphed
that they found they *could* come after all,
and the fourth accepted long ago, and
they've all sent flowers, so I can't very
well refuse, and the cards are all mixed
up dreadfully, and Emily feels *so* disgusted and blue!"

"Haven't you got a man yourself?" interrupted Biscuits, suspiciously. Miss Endicott was not in the habit of filling vacancies in this obliging manner and she was not at all fond of Evelyn, so it could not be a purely friendly office.

Suzanne clasped her hands tragically and assumed a Bernhardt attitude.

"Alas! I had. But his name was George. I loathe that name. *Mais que voulez-vous?* I did not know it till too late! I was sick with rage. It was to weep! I dismissed him. *Me voilà libre!*"

They giggled irrepressibly, for she was very funny. But Biscuits fastened her keen brown eyes on Suzanne's elusive blue ones and returned to the attack.

"Don't be idiotic, Suzanne—where's your man?"

Suzanne sighed sepulchrally.

"Ah, where? *Je l'ignore absolument,*

moi! Possibly he has drowned himself.
'Twere better so. It is awful to be blond
and named George! I telegraphed him
that I had sprained my ankle and
was desolated, but his sincerely. He
sent violets. So that I can take the
Prince.''

They looked helplessly at each other.
It might be just as she had said. She was
quite capable of it. And just because
she was the last person one would have
chosen to ask to take Emily Thayer's
fiancé to the Prom, she had, naturally
enough, offered to do it.

''Well,'' said Biscuits, doubtfully, ''I
suppose if you say you will, you will.
But I hope you won't do anything foolish.''

''Of course she won't,'' Evelyn broke
in hastily, ''and it's perfectly grand she
can take him, I'm sure. He's a right

nice man, too, Suzanne. He doesn't talk much but he's quite handsome, and Emily says he dances well.''

"That's more than she does,'' remarked Suzanne sweetly. "Oh, yes, Louisa, look kindly and begin to perjure yourself—it becomes a junior president, we all know! But on the two occasions when I had the pleasure we didn't seem to be performing the same dance at all, I assure you—it was most confusing. How long is she *fiancée?*''

"Oh, long before she came up here. It was arranged by the families, I guess. She's always known him. Could you—could you take care of him from now on, Suzanne dear? You could go out the side door and get your things on, and I'd wait here and take you down and introduce him—he's in the reception-room.''

Suzanne raised her eyebrows. "*Eh*

20

bien! Suppose I go now? And in costume? These foreigners always expect
so much,'' she said, lightly.

"In costume?" repeated Evelyn,
vaguely. Suzanne slipped off her shirt-
waist and produced from Biscuits' closet
a pink and gray kimono of soft crêpe.
She tied the long pink sash high under
her arms and before they quite realized
what she was doing she had piled her soft
straight hair in great puffs on her head
and stuck a lacquered paper-knife, shaped
like a dagger, between the coils. From
the chiffonier she took a string of amber
beads that she twisted about her wrist
and a long thin gold watch chain that she
looped about her forehead so that the little fob hung down between her eyes.
Three great red paper poppies hung over
the mirror, and as she slipped them
through her belt, and throwing her

21

weight on one hip, looked at them through slanted eyes, the glass reflected the most charmingly *bizarre* little figure in the world.

"*Très chic, n'est-ce pas?*" she said, opening the door. "I'll get E. Harper's mandolin and some bangles. *En avant,* Evelyn!"

"Why, Suzanne, where are you going? You're not going to meet Mr. Edwards—"

"*Comme ça?* Precisely."

She ran across the hall, to return with a beautiful little inlaid mandolin and a handful of tinkling silver bracelets. She had poised a great pink rose just over her forehead and held three more loosely in her hands; three others took the place of the poppies.

Biscuits caught her hand. "See here, Suzanne, you can't go down to the reception-room like this—you're a crazy child!''

Suzanne made a little face and twisted away. They chased after her to the head of the stairs and caught her, when they held her firmly, half laughing, half in earnest; expostulating, reproving, admiring.

"Oh, let her go!" said Evelyn, suddenly. "She's just doing it to tease us, Biscuits. She'll come back! And I *must* get away now, myself, after she's met him—let her go! She'll come right back, won't you, Suzanne? She won't go in.''

Suzanne began to pick the mandolin strings and sing softly. She was a naughty, bewitching child; it was impossible to resist her.

She slipped down the stairs with Evelyn beside her, the others following.

Down below it was utterly deserted. The unnatural quiet of a quiet campus house hung over everything. It was a perfect day and every one was reveling in it. At the farthest end of the long parlor sat a broad-shouldered, handsome boy, staring wearily out at the merry groups that passed and separated. He looked up, and catching sight of Evelyn rose politely, while the girls behind the portière gripped each others' hands in excitement as Suzanne quietly walked in beside her.

For a moment Evelyn hesitated. Then, with an expressive shrug of her shoulders for the group behind, she led the way to the boy. She was very anxious about her own affairs and far too self-centred to be much concerned at the probability of disastrous criticism if Suzanne's freak should become known.

24

"Miss Endicott," she said quickly, "allow me to present Mr. Edwards. Mr. Edwards—Miss Endicott!"

The boy bit his lip. He felt that there was some trick in progress and he stiffened his shoulders and said somewhat gruffly:

"Happy to meet you, I'm sure!" Then a strange feeling came to him, for with a suppleness he had never seen the slim pink and gray figure bowed till the great rose on her forehead touched the floor, and above a faint tinkle of bangles and a little jarring cry from the mandolin a soft *trainante* voice murmured:

"*Monseigneur!*"

Evelyn caught a suppressed giggle from behind the portière and glanced nervously around.

"Come!" she said shortly. Then turning to the boy: "We'll soon be back, Mr.

Edwards. I shall have to keep a previous engagement, but Miss Endicott—"

She stopped, for he was paying no attention to her. Indeed he had begun a speech of some sort to Suzanne, who drooped again to the carpet.

"*Mais je suis ravie, je vous assure, Monseigneur*—the honor, it is mine!" she cooed; then straightening again she looked him full in the face for a second.

"Shall I sing?" she asked.

"Goodness, no!" said Evelyn, sharply. But the boy advanced a step.

"Oh, yes, do sing!" he urged boldly. He had heard the giggle, too, and he was not going to be placidly made a fool of: he would bluff the thing out.

What she would sing he did not know. Emily sang a song called The Holy City, Sunday afternoons on her vacations, and at other times she sang The Rosary; her

friends all sang it, too; he connected it
vaguely with girls as a class. Still, he
had an instinct that she would not sing
The Rosary; though he had never seen
anything like her and thought her far
from pretty—he had a theory that large
blonde girls with violet eyes and pink
cheeks were technically pretty—he dimly
realized a personality in that little pink
and gray creature that startled him with
its poignancy. He wondered what she
would sing.

He looked at the piano seat, but she
sank on the floor at his feet, and throwing
back one sleeve with a clink of bracelets
and a gush of perfume from the heavy
roses, she struck a shrill, sweet chord
from the little lute-shaped thing in her
hand. The silence was absolutely tense.
A great bar of sunlight fell across her
bare, round arm; the rest of the room lay

in shadow. A strange little minor tune
wove itself among the tremulous chords,
a low vibrating voice chanted fascinating
syllables to it.

He caught her eyes fixed mournfully
on his; her head drooped over the mandolin; the May wind drove the roses in
sweet elusive gusts across his face.

"Colinette était son nom—"

The rest of the room faded; there were
no other girls; there was only a wonder-
ful, troubling dusky face that smelt of
roses; two long, gray-violet eyes that
looked through his own, beyond, to
France, and a sweet old tragedy there.

"Ce n'était qu'une fillette,
Je n'étais qu'un écolier,
Elle est morte en février—
Pauvre Colinette!"

28

HER FIANCÉ

It seemed to him that the room had suddenly grown warm, that all the East of the Arabian Nights was there, all the romance that he had heard of but never understood. That little break in her voice—how it made one catch one's breath! That chain through her hair—how taking it was! He had never noticed that women wore such things in their hair. And how soft and pale her arms were, where the sleeve fell back; how sweet she was, all crouched together below his chair—one could pick her up so easily—

"Elle est morte en février, en février—"

Ah, that little break again!

"Pauvre Colinette!"

The hall door opened; a babble of voices filled the rooms. She slipped to

her feet in a second, lithe as a cat. Again
the low, drooping bow, the murmured:

"Monseigneur!"

She was in the hall and gone. The
mandolin struck against the stairs as she
ran up and the little faint clang of the
wires was the last sigh of Colinette.

He did not hear the remonstrance of
the girls; their laughter, half admiration,
half nervousness; their excited assur-
ances that nobody in the world but Suzanne would have been permitted such a
clear coast by Providence—that anybody
else would inevitably have been haled
forth out of the parlor; their disgusted
queries of what in the world Mr. Edwards
would think; their voluble doubt as to
what she was going to do now—how she
would explain herself to him.

In all the hot tumult of his thoughts one
rang out like a clear bell: if all those other

30

things were girls, what was this? If this
was a girl, what were they? He had
never been a girl's boy: he had boated
and tramped and fished, and trained for
various elevens, and got his lessons and
lived with the fellows. He was very
popular with them; he knew many of
them very intimately. Out of friendship
for them he had filled dozens of programs
and paddled dozens of girls about in
canoes. Some girls danced heavily and
tilted the boat and giggled; some chattered and asked too many questions;
some wore too much perfume. Many
whom the fellows raved over he realized
were extremely pretty—he observed that
they realized it, too. His experience had
led him to infer that dark girls were liable
to be cleverer than light ones, and that
stout girls danced very well as a usual
thing.

HER FIANCÉ

From the days of his short trousers he had known that he was going to marry Emily. His mother and hers had been lifelong friends and their fathers had been college chums and were practically business partners. They lived in the same street in the city and their country places touched, with not even a hedge between. If any one had asked him just when he fell in love with Emily he would have looked puzzled and said that they'd always known each other. If he had been asked to describe his proposal, it is almost certain that his mind would have rested comfortably on that occasion when his father had looked somewhat anxiously over his cigar and said earnestly:

"I've never had any fault to find with you, Al, and if you can see your way to this, my boy, you'd make your mother and me perfectly contented. It's all we

32

could ask, all. You—you love her, don't
you, Al?''

''Why, certainly, sir!'' he had said,
and then they had discussed the plans for
the new stables.

There would be a large wing added for
them when they were married, and afterward, ''when we old folks are gone, Al,''
the places would be thrown together—
there would be a large estate then.

He had never come up to see Emily
before. He saw her every vacation with
the rest of the family, and then, Smith
girls never paraded their engagements,
she said. Most people didn't announce
them till junior year and kept quiet
about them after that. College wasn't
the place for that sort of thing; if you
wanted a lot of that you were a fool to
come.

There was enough to occupy you without an interest presumably so absorbing as to stale the other pleasures before you'd really exhausted them. Cornelia Burt had said, somewhat successfully, that at college it was perfectly legitimate to be interested in *men,* but very foolish to become attached to *a man.*

He had met Miss Burt; she was one of the dark kind that are clever and he had been a little afraid of her—he found nothing to say. Miss Lyon had chattered so steadily that he had hardly felt it necessary to pay attention. She had told him the names of all the buildings and he had said, "Ah! Is it?" and tried to look the way she pointed. He was neither pleased nor displeased, dull nor amused. He had the placid content of perfect health and strength; he liked to walk on the soft grass, and the air was sweet and fresh. He expected to meet Johnson, of

34

his class, somewhere up here, and Johnson could tell him if the courts had been
rolled yet and when he was likely to get
a chance at them.

And now—something had happened.
His calm, vague interest in life had been
ruffled suddenly, disturbed; his custom-
ary attitude of waiting till the next thing
happened had utterly changed; he wanted
something to come and come immediately
—he wanted that girl to come back. He
had never been taken out of himself
before; he had never known the fascination of floating helplessly in the sea of his
own emotions; he had an idea that he
would see better what he wanted when
she came.

When she appeared in the door a thing
occurred to him that he had experienced
only once in his life, when he had been
coming in well ahead in a boat race and

just at the finish had felt the shell behind
him suddenly dart half a length ahead.
His heart appeared to drop down out of
its place and he pumped it up with a
tremendous breath that brought the blood
surging to his forehead. She was dressed
in something sheer and ruffled, of a mar-
velous blue; not violet or gray or grape-
colored, or a real blue at all, in fact, but
only to be classified when she turned her
eyes on him. Then he saw that the dress
was the color of Suzanne. In her belt
were heavy, deep-pink roses; he would
never think of them apart from her
again.

They left the house and walked about
among the groups and couples, and when
he heard her answer he knew that he had
spoken. She had a great power of
silence; not comfortable, comradely
silence, like Emily's, born of a common

36

experience, a familiar past, a settled
future; but a mysterious, sweet silence
that meant everything he was thinking
and more beyond.

He did not know that she could chatter
like a magpie, that her usual conversation
was a monologue with casual interrup-
tions, that her wit spared no one and
often hurt the very person who brought
it out. This low-voiced, withdrawn,
slender blue thing was as wrapped up in
her new personality as he was.

> *"Colinette était son nom,*
> *Elle habitait un village."*

They sat on a bench under an apple
tree and he talked to her about himself;
he hardly realized that this was something he rarely did. When she replied,
that little minor tone crept into his heart

and echoed there; it was time to go so
soon!

They took supper with a gay party at
the girls' lunch-room, and it seemed to
him that he and she were the only real
people in the laughing, chattering crowd.
The red candle shades, the table carna-
tions, the bustling waitresses, the inces-
sant clatter of the small tables from which
high screens divided their large one,
seemed the merest theatrical background
for her small figure, the merest accom-
paniment to her low voice.

Johnson was opposite him and leaned
over in one of the pauses to ask if he
knew the courts were ready.

"What courts? Ah, yes, are they?"
he answered vaguely.

The girls who had told their men about
the amusing Miss Endicott raised their
eyebrows at each other.

"What's the matter with Suzanne? Doesn't she feel well?" they asked.

"She was well enough this afternoon," said Evelyn. "She's just taken a streak, that's all. I do hope she'll be decent to Emily's man—you can't trust her one hour."

She had on a long, light party cloak when he took her over to the gymnasium, and when it was thrown off and he saw the same dress she had worn in the afternoon he did not know enough to feel surprised. Only when his eye was caught by a silver chain on her thin, white neck did he remember that there was a blue ribbon there before and that her shoulders had been covered up. Nodding against her soft skin were pink roses; a silver comb was in her hair.

At the door an usher stopped them. "No flowers on the floor, please," she

39

said.   Suzanne looked her full in the
face.   Her eyes were almost sorrowful.

"These flowers are artificial!" she
murmured.

The girl's eyes widened.   Her face fell.
"Oh!" she gasped, "excuse me!" and
Suzanne passed on.

"Where do you think I shall go when I
die?" she asked him gravely.

He thought her utterly enchanting.

"Somewhere that I can come!" he said
boldly.

He paid no attention to the decora-
tions; the great red poppies, the green
boughs, the twined cheesecloth, the walls
hung with bagdads and posters, the
shaded lamps, the puffy cushions, the
brass and copper that gleamed from dull
corners, the palms and ferns that softened the angles.   It might as well have
been a barn.

40

HER FIANCÉ

He looked at his card; Emily had six dances. The extras were vacant.

"May I have all the extras?" he asked in a matter-of-fact tone. How he did it he never knew.

She smiled and rested her eyes on his. "If you really dance well," she said lightly.

He got through the dances with the others mechanically. He knew nothing about them at the time, but when he came back to her and she leaned against his shoulder he felt that they had been awkward and tightly dressed; most of them were too big. When the fresh, strong odor of the pink roses came to him he remembered that they all smelled of violet extract. Her little cool bare hand in his taught him that theirs had been hot and gloved.

He had danced with girls before, but

41

when he put his arm around her it occurred to him for the first time in his life that to dance with a woman was to take her in one's arms. How close to his face her soft hair rose and fell! She breathed very lightly, but he could have counted her breaths. He had never danced before—he had simply kept time to music. He found himself thinking aloud to her.

"You don't push me and try to lead, like some of them, and you don't pull away when *I* lead," he explained.

She smiled inscrutably. She was probably the best dancer in the college—certainly no one danced better.

"I don't talk when I dance—what's the use?" She swayed nearer him and slipped aside again. He guided her easily through the swishing, whirling crowd: she had no skirt to hold up, no fan for him to carry, no high-twisted thing

42

sticking up in her hair that got in his way.

When he gave her up to another man he tried not to watch him put an arm around her to start away with her—it irritated him unspeakably. When she came back to him the evening grew sweet again, the music swelled richer; he sighed as if he had not quite breathed before, and held her firmly.

As the night wore on Suzanne spoke less and less. She closed her eyes when she danced; her lips parted a little. A faint pink came into her cheeks and she leaned closer against his shoulder. The violins seemed to him like human voices; he found himself humming the airs under his breath as he led her through the crowd. He had never noticed the dance music before; he thought they played beautifully to-night.

43

Later he found himself on the steps of
her house with her cloak over his arm.
The strains of the last waltz rose above
the surf-like roll of the feet and voices.
They were quite alone. Her eyelids
drooped, her lips half smiled, her head
swayed a little to the music. She gave
him her hand and leaned down toward
him.

"Good-night," she said.

He drew her hand higher, and with an
absolutely novel impulse kissed the back
of it. She laughed softly and left him.

"Adieu—mon cher Prince!"

She had taken the cloak from him, but
as he passed out of the wide gateway he
realized that he clutched a long-stemmed
pink rose in his hand.

That night as he walked hour after
hour through the deserted streets it grew
slowly clear to him. This was what they

meant, those fellows at whose weddings
he had ushered! This was the way that
man in Henry Esmond felt—he had taken
a course in English literature, in his
sophomore year, and had read the pre-
scribed novels mechanically—he did not
care for reading. So this was it: no
wonder they made such a fuss about it! It
hurt you, really hurt you. And yet it was
far from disagreeable—you wouldn't lose
it for the world. To take her away, to
have her all the time—why, that meant
to marry her! Certainly, that was what
he would do: marry her. And *he* would
have ushers and a breakfast . . . great
heavens! He was going to marry Emily!

He was sitting on a little porch near an
electric light when he next realized his
surroundings, staring at a swarm of flies
that eddied around it. How absurd!
How entirely ridiculous! That large,

comfortable girl he had known all his life
—marry her! *Marry her!* Why, what
would he care if he never saw her again?
There was only one girl in the world that
he would ever marry. She was slender
and soft, and smelt of roses.

In the morning he wrote a letter to
Emily in his big, boyish hand explaining
the situation. He would willingly have
seen her, but she was still in bed, and
though convalescent, unable to see any
one. They had become engaged, he said,
under a misunderstanding; he didn't
think they quite realized what a serious
matter it was to marry—anybody. It
was a good thing he had found out in
time. They would talk it over in the
summer, but he was sure she would agree
with him. Really, to be awfully fond of
anybody, and all that, wasn't quite
enough—there was a great deal more to

it—it was hard to explain, but they'd talk it over in the summer. He supposed it would be a hard slam for father, but father shouldn't have been so certain he knew what was best. He hoped she'd be better soon, and was hers as ever, Al.

He was quite pleased with her reply, and wished the others would be as sensible. He was only twenty-two, and he had never felt anything in his life before, so he devoted himself diligently to feeling this, and was as unconscious as a Newfoundland puppy of the things he tore up during the weeks in which he taught his family that they had never known him. He regretted that Emily's health seemed to demand the Maine woods. He would have liked to talk things over with her—he was more used to talking with her than with any one else feminine, and she would be apt to know

47

more of Suzanne. He could not understand why her mother should blow her nose whenever he inquired after Emily, and he thought his father displayed a frothy kind of temper that did not particularly become him.

For the next few weeks he worked hard, pushing off all the time a delightful, vague future. Something lurked behind written papers, something made him rest on his oars and drift, something made long, solitary walks seem short and pleasant, something set him humming to himself and smiling at nothing. There was no hurry. He would wait till after Commencement and find her in the summer. He had never been disappointed in his life.

To his surprise, he got on a car one day and stayed in till it reached Northampton. This he had not planned, and it startled him to find that he was hurrying up the main street at a pace to attract attention. He made his dressing an occasion for much thought and time, and reached her house just at dusk.

He sat alone in the reception-room, and for fifteen minutes knew the most crowded happiness, the sweetest, hottest tumult of his young life. Would she glide in between the curtains? How had she drawn him to her—what had made him come before he knew?

The maid stood before him. Miss Endicott begged to be excused to-night. She was going out of town—abroad—in a few days. She was very busy indeed.

He stared incredulously at her. Abroad? Why—she had sent for him—

"It's rather important," he said in his firm, matter-of-fact way, "and I only want to see her a little while. I can wait. See if she can see me later, perhaps."

HER FIANCÉ

He did not know if it was ten minutes
or half an hour before Evelyn Lyon appeared.

"Why, Mr. Edwards, how nice!" she
chattered. "I knew it was you. Miss
Endicott's coming down for just a few
minutes if you'll excuse her later. She's
going abroad in three days—leaving
early, you see, and dreadfully rushed, of
course. She wouldn't have sent you
away, but she didn't know who you were
at first: she thought it was another Mr.
Edwards we know—a Williams man—
I'm afraid," archly, "she'd forgotten
you just a little!"

This was to punish him for letting his
face fall as he saw her, but he did not
know it, and scowled a little.

"I should have telegraphed," he said
stiffly.

"Well, yes," she admitted, "it's safer.

You see, an artist friend of her brother's
—he lives in Paris—is in this country
and he came right up here to see her.
He's coming at eight. Suzanne's crazy
over Paris, you know—she used to live
there. She's quite excited over going.
You didn't know about it?''

There was a swish of skirts, a patter
of high heels on bare floor, and Suzanne
was in the room. Something ruffled and
smoke-colored, with thin, thin sleeves and
a transparent neck, turned her eyes soft
gray, but a great bunch of heliotrope at
her belt showed you that they were really
blue-violet if she liked. A faint, soft
pink burned in her cheeks; she smiled
vaguely at the room. Her hair was coiled
low and pulled down over her ears—
one would no more have expected her to
carry a mandolin than a shepherdess'
crook.

51

HER FIANCÉ

"So glad to see you, Mr. er-Edwards," she said rapidly, "and so sorry to have kept you waiting. Miss Lyon has explained about my going—yes? And my engagement at eight—*très bien!* I am horribly rushed. I wish you might have come before. Is Emily well? She's coming back next year, *n'est-ce pas?* Too bad she broke down. She's up on Elm Street yet, I suppose? Ah, is she? I didn't know; when did she go? Then you're not up to see her? *Ah, fi donc! Est-ce possible!*"

He felt very much as he did when the trainer poured on cold water when he didn't expect it, and wouldn't stop. Who was this girl? He felt very young, very awkward, very tired, suddenly.

Some one entered the little room. Suzanne looked prettier than most really pretty women, and held out both hands.

HER FIANCÉ

A tall, dark man bowed low over them
and murmured quickly in French:

"Enchanté de l'honneur—"

"Charmée de vous voir—"

He felt as if he were at a play. This
vivid, brilliant creature—who was she?
Where was his soft-eyed, quiet lady of
pink roses?

She turned with a fascinating little
laugh to the two in the background and
introduced them to the stranger—*"c'est
un de mes vieux amis!"*

For one sweet, hurting second she
smiled into the tall boy's eyes—the smile
he knew. *"Je vous prie de m'excuser,"*
she murmured softly, then recollecting
herself, in English: "He comes from
my brother. I—I think you know Miss
Lyon best up here? Or was it Miss
Burt? Either, I am sure, would be glad
to do anything—*Au revoir!*"

53

HER FIANCÉ

His hand was empty—she was across the room. She looked back and smiled again.

"Adieu! à plus tard, peut-être—"

"Shall we walk around the campus a little?" said Evelyn, perfunctorily. It was just like Suzanne to leave this sulky youth on her hands.

Around and around the narrow, winding paths they went—for how long he never knew. Evelyn talked and he grew up very fast, and hoped he wasn't showing how horribly it hurt him. He had never been hit like this before, and he breathed hard and wondered if he'd feel this way long. He felt very sorry for the poor fool of a boy that had thought such idiotic things on the train: he hoped she hadn't any idea. Oh, where was it gone, all that sweet, vague future? How damnably empty it was—what did it matter, anyhow? He'd go and—ah, was that how Jack Hunter felt when the little red-headed DeLong girl threw him over? He used to wake people up at night and beg them to take walks—

"Why, isn't that Suzanne? Hush— don't tell them we're here. Isn't it funny we both came here?" whispered Evelyn.

Under a big tree on the upper Para-dise path sat Suzanne, holding a man-dolin. At her feet was her brother's friend.

The two underneath them could see their faces quite plainly in the moonlight. The boy realized that he had been hear-ing the tune for some time—it had driven his thoughts back over the old sweet road, it had filled his heart to the brim. In the still night air the words came plainly:

HER FIANCÉ

"Un tel récit est bien vieux;
Cette histoire est bien commune,
Pourtant il n'en est pas une
Qui ne mouille pas les yeux."

"Isn't that a fascinating little tune?" said Evelyn, "she made it up herself."

He put his hand in his pocket; later, a faded brown rose dropped into the undergrowth of the lower Paradise path. Evelyn heard a little, short laugh and thought she must have said something funny. Later, she remembered that she hadn't spoken for some time—they had walked steadily for an hour—and decided that he was a rude, thoughtless boy.

In this opinion she was but partly right. Rude he was, certainly, but he had never been more thoughtful in his life; and had she only known it, she had never walked in Paradise with a less boyish boy.

"SHE HAD NEVER WALKED IN PARADISE WITH A LESS BOYISH BOY"

HER LITTLE SISTER

HER LITTLE SISTER

THE baby began crying for the third time in an hour, and Lydia jumped from her hastily snatched book to comfort him. She sat by his crib with one accustomed, maternal finger thrust between the bars, and remarked occasionally to him as he nibbled and sucked at it: "Well, well! did he wake up, then? So he did!" Under the influence of this soothing monologue he drifted off to sleep again, and she returned triumphantly, to meet the somewhat cynical gaze of her younger sister.

Cornelia lay back comfortably on five assorted cushions, one hand dangling conveniently near a bowl of grapes, the other marking her place in the Jungle Book.

"When are you going to let Thekla quiet him when he howls?" she inquired, disapprovingly.

"He won't stop for Thekla. You know he won't," his mother replied proudly, "and he was not howling, Neal; he just wanted to know I was around. I can stop him so easily, and Thekla is ironing now; besides she hates to be disturbed when she is doing fine work."

"She can't very well be disturbed by those handkerchiefs, if that is what you mean by 'fine work,' for you did them yourself yesterday afternoon. And it is no matter anyhow if she does hate to be disturbed. That's what she's paid for. I don't like to be disturbed myself, but if I were paid sixteen dollars a month and my board for it, I should expect to be."

60

HER LITTLE SISTER

Lydia smiled tolerantly. "When you have servants yourself," she said, "you will understand a little better, my dear. I can do the handkerchiefs much better than she can, for that matter, and Dick is so particular about his handkerchiefs."

"He is particular about his dessert, too, I notice," Cornelia remarked, "but I doubt very much if I should be willing to get my face all red, and drop a spoonful of butter on my best black skirt in order to satisfy his particularity in that regard."

Again Lydia smiled. "When you are married, my dear," she said, "you will feel very differently about a great many things. And the spot came out, besides."

"But it was you that got it out, and you worked all the afternoon over it, and you couldn't go to drive with us. You don't get out half enough, Sis, and you promised mother that you'd go for an hour every day.''

At this point, a resounding yell from the nursery, where little Cornelia was occupied in knocking her sister down and walking over her, interrupted matters, and Lydia ran up the stairs to rescue the oppressed and discipline the oppressor, remaining to superintend their funny little luncheon, spread out in due state on the sewing table, where silver mugs and alphabet plates made a brave showing, and little food pushers learned to lie straight in fat fingers. They were delicious babies, and devoted to their mother. She listened with her never failing interest to their lurid account of the morning's adventures, lectured at length on the essential differences between food pushers and the ordinary teaspoon of society, wiped the milk from their round chins and kissed them ecstatically as they rolled questioning eyes at her over the rims of the silver mugs. After luncheon they begged for a story, and with one on either knee, she had begun The Three Bears, when a thundering rap on the door and a hurried invitation to luncheon brought her flying down the two flights of stairs, with a guilty consciousness of that lateness at meals which so annoyed her in other people. With her hand on the knob of the dining room door, she was already a little way in her apologies, when it occurred to her that they were neither of them listening to her.

Neal, a spot of sunshine in her bright scarlet blouse, was serving Dick, whose laughter at some one of her college tales entirely drowned the late comer's voice.

Lydia paused a moment in the door to push back her loose hair, and as Dick

leaped from his seat to pick up Neal's
fallen napkin, it occurred to her that the
little courtesy surprised her. She remembered with a sudden flush of pleasure
how on their wedding journey she had
dropped her napkin once, twice, three
times, and Dick had handed it to her
kneeling, and she had redeemed it with a
kiss. That was four years ago: was it
possible he had never picked up her napkin since? She pushed through the doorway with a quick feeling of discontent,
and dropped into Neal's place, for her
own was taken.

"Ah! here you are," said Dick, "late
again, as usual. We have kept you one
sardine. And do you mean to say that
the professor was satisfied with that explanation, Neal? Does a man necessarily become imbecile when he undertakes
to train the female mind?"

"He does not necessarily become imbecile when he begins to train it, but after a while his reason is apt to totter, and on this occasion it tottered to its fall, like the Roman empire, because he actually believed her."

Lydia was conscious of an intense and unreasonable irritation. "Judy is better this morning," she said abruptly.

Her husband looked up in surprise. "Why! what's the matter with her?" he inquired, easily. "I didn't know she was sick. Did you have the doctor in?"

Lydia bit her lip nervously. "If it had been a case for the doctor," she said, in the restrained voice adopted by a woman who has been doing, on an average, four different things an hour for three hours, "you would certainly have heard of it before. She was merely a little feverish."

"And Sis gave her aconite, belladonna, and bryonia, or some more of those little pellets out of the red case," Neal added, laughing. "It's my belief they are numbered one, two, three, four, up to ten, and she uses them in regular order, irrespective of the complaint of the infant in question." The father of the infant in question laughed heartily, too heartily, it seemed to Lydia, and she flashed a sudden look at him. He caught it and watched her curiously.

"Why, what's the matter?" he asked, "what makes you so flushed? You look as if you had run a mile." His glance slipping down her figure made her uncomfortably conscious of her loose dressing sack, with its informal sleeves, and as she ran her fingers nervously through her hair, her color rose.

Neal seemed to her at that moment

unbearably fresh and trim, her waist too well defined, her shoulders too broad and smoothly fitted. The little scarlet bow in her hair, that matched her waist—this correspondence was a fad of Neal's—struck her suddenly as coquettish and a little vulgar. And her voice, when she spoke, rang too impersonally, too free from worry, too insultingly at ease.

"Sis came leaping down the stairs much too fast," she remarked, "having bounded up at a pace I have rarely seen equaled. It borders a little too much on the strenuous life for me."

Dick scowled a little. "If Hall has told you once not to run up and down those stairs, he has told you twenty times," he said shortly. "Can't you send one of the girls?"

"Your views on the care of children coincide remarkably with Neal's." Her

67

voice was cold and indifferent. "It is a pity that the experience of both of you is so limited—it rather detracts from the value of your advice."

They stared at her a moment and Dick turned to Cornelia. "That is along the lines of a 'squelch,' is it not?" he inquired. "I seem to grasp the force of the idiom as never before."

"It's a very good example," she returned with a laugh; "on　ets used to them at college. Just think that in a little more than two months I shall be all through with it!"

The talk ran on and Lydia heard it vaguely, almost as through a dream. She heard Neal describe her house party at the beach after commencement, her subsequent round of visits with college friends, her plans for the winter. Dick cordially approved of them all.

"Of course," she found herself thinking, "of course it's 'all right' and 'a
good scheme.' Anything Neal does is all
right. Presently someone will offer her
the editorship of the Atlantic Monthly if
she wants it—she always gets what she
wants."

Suddenly they jumped up from the
table.

"Good heavens! that car goes at 2.05!"
he cried. "Are you all ready, Nealie? I
left my driver at the shop for repairs, and
we'll have to stop for it. Look lively,
now, and we'll get it yet. Good-by, dear,
I left that vest on the bed. If Hall should
drop in, send him on to the links—good-
by!"

The hall door closed behind them.
Through the open window of the parlor
she heard his voice as they stepped off
briskly, the golf bag clanking between
them. 69

HER FIANCE

"Thank the Lord you don't have to stop half an hour prinking! Some girls, now—"

"And she spent half an hour, exactly, doing her hair—what a fool a man is!" Lydia said aloud. "No, I don't want any dessert, Thekla, you may take the things."

She walked slowly up the stairs and sat down by the window. She had an impulse to throw the sash up and sit for a moment in the warming spring air, but the sight of the children running toward her checked it, and she rested her hot forehead against the pane. Though Judy clambered half way to her waist and little Cornelia shrieked out the finale of The Three Bears in a high accusatory treble, she answered them only half consciously.

It was taken for granted, then, that she

should sit at home and sew. No one suspected that she might like to put on a neat
short skirt and a red blouse and walk
for the afternoon over the breezy links.
No one considered that a cup of tea in the
little club house and a chat with the merry
company might freshen her as well as
her husband. She could stay alone. But
even as a hot tear slipped down her cheek
and splashed on the sill her honest brain
refused its sympathy. It was impossible
for her to forget that Dick had urged her
to join the club with him. She could not
but remember how Dr. Hall had coaxed
her to learn to play, three years ago,
when Judy was born.

"It will keep you out of doors, my
dear," he had urged, "and make an outside interest for you. This outdoor fad
is a great thing, whether you young
wives feel superior or not! Walk over

71

to the club house and get him, anyway!"

She had done it for one season, and they had walked home together—what jolly chats they used to have! But the children came quickly, little Neal was delicate, and there had been so much sewing. She had slipped out of it in the first cold weather, though the doctor had scolded her, and Dick was used to the car now.

She picked up Burt's new dress, a sheer white thing, all foaming with ruffles, and began the tiny buttonholes. They were a family of dainty needlewomen: she had secretly rejoiced in her superiority over Neal in this line of accomplishment, when the younger sister had given up such work under the pressure of college life. But last summer she had suddenly taken it in hand again and Lydia was obliged

to confess that neither golf, canoeing nor
the dissection of frogs had coarsened the
fairy stitches that Neal set in her name-
sake's little frocks. After all, what had
she gained in the three or four years that
Neal had wasted, from her sister's point
of view, in what she had supposed at first
to be an exclusively educational experience? Great social training? But since
her marriage she had almost given up her
old school friends and their amusements,
and Cornelia had, in her various visits
and her encounters with the many different types of a large college, seen more of
the world than she. She had not kept up
her music, while Neal had not only gained
for herself a collegiate reputation as a
writer, but had actually turned her year
of college editorship to account and was
practically engaged as assistant reader
on one of the "nearly first-rate maga-

zines,'' as she expressed it. Lydia had learned through the necessities of four years' housekeeping to defend herself against the utter desolation of an occasionally cookless kitchen; but Cornelia, from a long course of chafing-dish suppers and Sunday morning breakfasts, could boast a more varied culinary repertoire, and, as her sister admitted, had managed the house very capably during the last vacation, when Lydia carried Judy through scarlatina.

In the flush of her honeymoon she had scoffed at Neal's firmly expressed intention to refuse all proposals to marry, ''even if he should be a duke,'' till she was twenty-four; but now she caught herself wondering if Neal had not been wiser.

''To stop everything at twenty-one''— she broke her thought off sharply. What a dreadful thing! Stop? Why, she had only begun. What were all these plans and pleasures and freedoms to her precious nursery three? And Dick—but again that dull, scornful pain settled over her heart, and she saw his interested face turned toward Cornelia, heard his ''Are you all ready, Nealie?'' and pressed her lips together.

The needle flashed through Burt's buttonholes. The babies wore nothing but white, and the work on their little garments was the marvel and despair of her friends. All the skill and time that went once to her own girlish fineries were lavished on their plump persons, and when they stood at the foot of the stairs, three tucked and ruffled snowdrifts, to welcome father home, she forgot, as who does not forget, the sacrifices to her weakness, the hours of patient stitching and the many self-imposed tasks in the kitchen that placated a wearied laundress.

To-day she sewed as a man rows against the current to tire himself into a dreamless sleep. Her cheeks grew hot and flushed, her lips were drawn hard. The children played quietly by themselves. She tried to forget how Dick and Neal used to beg her to leave them to Thekla and come out.

"But they do not want me now! They do not!" she reiterated, stooping to catch the waning light.

"Why, Lydia Sherrill! Put up that work this minute! It's dark as pitch!"

She sat up dizzily. Neal swept through the room, dragging a great trail of fresh outdoors in with her.

"We had such a grand game! Dick's going in for the cup—did you know it? Do you know it's six o'clock? You

76

might just as well have come out with
me and made those calls. Thekla says
she's had the babies for the last hour.
I'm going over to the Ryders' musicale
to-night—they're going to dance after-
wards.''

She lay back in the sewing chair. Her
eyes ached miserably and in a sudden
nervous tremor she flung Burt's little
white frock across the floor. She seemed
to hear Dick's quizzical laugh.

''Oh, what's the difference, dear, so
long as they're clean? There's more
lace than baby!''

Neal was splashing in the tub. ''Can
you wait dinner till quarter of seven?''
she called. ''I'll be ready then, Sis.''

Her voice sounded dry and hard even
to herself as she answered: ''I will speak
to Frederika, but hurry, please. I promised Thekla she could go early to-night.''

77

Dick appeared in the doorway struggling with a refractory stud. "For heaven's sake, Lydia, do get over your unreasonable awe of those girls! If we can't put off dinner fifteen minutes—"

"It isn't that, but I promised her, Dick," she explained gently, her chin quivering. She put her hand on his arm. If only he would hold her close and make her forget this terrible afternoon!

"Oh, Lord, there it goes again! I'll tie it on with a string!" he muttered, and she went quickly to the kitchen.

The dining room seemed to glare with a hundred lights as she took her place behind the soup tureen.

"You're blinking like an owl, dear—what's the matter?" said Dick, "headache again? That's a shame—I wanted you to come over after the musicale and stay awhile before I bring Neal back—ah, *mes compliments, mademoiselle!''*

Neal was not a beautiful girl, she was hardly handsome; but she looked very striking in her white evening gown, with a bunch of daffodils against her soft bare shoulders, and an amber comb in her dark hair. Her cheeks were rosy with exercise; a faint violet perfume floated behind her as she swept them a deep courtesy and dropped into the chair Dick pulled out for her. A pleasant afternoon and a happy evening to come were plain in her face. She was in high spirits and entertained them with inexhaustible college nonsense. Dick roared at her jokes.

Lydia spoke as often as they spoke to her, but in her mind one sentence rang exclusively: ''I am jealous of my sister! I am jealous of my sister!''

As Neal prattled on, the older woman

79

looked at her curiously, as if through other eyes. The greatest difference between them was not, as she had always supposed, that Cornelia was the product of a somewhat doubtful system of higher education, while she represented the normal young woman; but it lay in the fact that Neal, who showed to the ordinary observer no signs whatever of any greater knowledge or culture than she herself possessed, was on the whole, a young woman of wide interests, many friends and acquaintances, much practical ability, and a certain *savoir faire*, while her sister, tired and worried, spent herself on three babies and two servants—

"You are spilling water on that brown silk waist, sister dear, but as I hate you in it, keep it up, and perhaps you'll throw it away," said Neal cordially.

80

HER LITTLE SISTER

"You ought to wear more white—white was very becoming to you. Women ought always to wear white," Dick announced, his eyes on the white gown at his left. Lydia caught his glance and tightened her lips. She hardly knew when they left the house.

In the middle of the evening she found herself in Neal's room, fingering the polished toilet things on the dresser. What dainty pins, what pretty bows, what a fascinating feminine shimmer of glass and silver! And Neal was not a bit rich—there was just enough for her and mother—but there had been many presents, of course. She herself had begged everybody to give her presents for the house and the children, and so of course, they had. And Judy had broken her mirror and little Neal had lost her manicure set and the baby dragged at the bureau scarf so, that she kept very little on it. She remembered that she had not put them to bed nor even said goodnight. Thekla had done it, and how quiet they were: they had not even called for her.

Her picture, taken just before her marriage, stood in a silver frame on Neal's bureau. Had she looked so much like Neal as that? Yes, her mother said they were like the same girl. Only she had been prettier—everybody said so. She was the pretty one and Neal was the bright one. And now—

She leaned against the mirror, the picture in her hand. She lost all count of time.

"Why, Sis! What are you doing? What made you take your waist off? Aren't you well? I made Dick come home early—"

"Was he so sorry to come?"

"Why—why, Lydia, what do you mean?"

"I mean that he seems fairly willing—"

"Lydia, the more you say to-night the sorrier you'll be to-morrow. You're sick. Don't talk any more till I get my waist off—this pin is killing me." She came presently and stood by the mirror, and at the sight of their twin reflection, Lydia broke into a short laugh.

"Quite a contrast, eh?" she said, sharply.

Neal's fresh round shoulders rose from a white foam of lace and ribbon; her hair was fluffed softly about her face, her cheeks were crimson. Her sister, though only three years older, looked far more. There were lines about her mouth and between her eyes; the soft curves of her neck had tightened and sharpened; her face was colorless.

"Quite a contrast," she repeated, staring into the glass. She was dimly conscious that if Neal should try to comfort her or kiss her, she must pour out all her miserable heart, and hate her afterward. But this Neal did not do.

"If you would leave the children sometimes and get out in the air," she said calmly, "there would be less contrast. If you would wave your hair as you used to, and take the ruffles and lace off the children's clothes and put them on your own white things, there would be less still. And if you would occasionally discuss something else beside the vagaries of Frederika, the performances of Burt and the management of the house generally, there would be none at all!"

Lydia looked at her doubtfully. "It

84

is my own affair—how I shall dress my children,'' she said.

''Oh, very well,'' Cornelia replied cheerfully. ''Suit yourself. If you wish to dress them like crown princesses, more or less, and go about in underclothes you wouldn't give a cook for a Christmas present, very well. But don't think you're pleasing your husband.''

''My husband didn't marry me for—''

''Your lingerie? Certainly not, but you were mighty particular about your wedding things, I notice.''

Lydia's mood was changing with every moment. She was no longer sick and hurt. She was angry and thrown on her mettle. Her eyes flashed.

''Your conception of the responsibilities of marriage—'' she began, but Neal interrupted.

''My conception of the chief responsibility would be to keep my husband's love and interest as long as I could," she said decidedly. "It wouldn't be how the table napkins were ironed nor whether Toots gained the right number of pounds every month. When you camped out in the flat that first year, and took what there was, and came out skating and riding with the rest of us, and sang to Dick, and went off over Sunday with him, you'd never have talked so to me. You'd never have needed to. Now, just because I remind him of how you used to be, and he wants somebody to play with—"

"What do you mean, Neal Burt?"

"Just what I say. If my husband liked me in white so much, I'd wear it, and wres... with Frederika for something worth while, and dress the babies in blue gingham—they're all right in anything. And I'd get fatter. Oh, yes, you can if

86

you want to—you did that summer, when you were engaged, when Dick was worried about you.'' She stopped suddenly, and bending over, kissed the tip of her sister's ear.

''This is all,'' she said, ''and I'll apologize if you like, but I hate to see you making a fool of yourself, Sis! Goodnight,'' and she half pushed, half led her to her own room.

Lydia never remembered quite accurately what happened during the next few days. She was very tired and listless and agreed to everything. She knew that Dick was going on a walking tour which the doctor said he needed, and she told him that she hoped it would do him good. She welcomed her mother to the house, kissed the babies good-by, and went with a trunk to a place where there were groves of musical pine trees and warm, sunned needles under foot. She slept a great deal and ate when she was not sleeping. She nodded to many people, and talked a little, and sat in the sun. She knew that she was an unhappy young woman who had made a mistake of some sort, but this troubled her less than she would have supposed.

And suddenly one morning she woke from a refreshing sleep into a sunny blue day, and was glad to be alive. Some tiresome cloud of long ago had slipped from her heart in the night, and she wondered at that vexed and doubtful woman who sent such stupid postal cards to her husband in the Adirondacks. She wrote him a long letter, telling him of the pines and the blue and the sunsets, and the books she was reading. And he wrote back that he was most anxious to come on, but that Dr. Hall had mentioned two weeks of strangers and solitude, and it was only half over. So Lydia sat in the sun another week, and toward the end of it she summoned Dr. Hall and told him that it was now time to see the babies and their father. He looked at her and smiled.

"Perhaps you're right," he said.

And in the evening as she sat at her window watching the pines and the rising stars, wondering how she should see him first, there was a tap at the door, a quick stride across the room, and she was in his arms.

"Sweetheart, your letters were so dear! They were like the old ones—I wanted to see you so! You are so lovely in the white gown—is it that one? Is that the tree you sat under? Are you glad to see me? Will you stay here a week with me—all by ourselves?"

89

"Yes—yes—yes," she whispered, conscious only of his kisses.

Later, as she wandered with him under the stars, in some strange, dreamy way a girl again, in Aunt Lydia's old orchard, she laughed softly, while he planned their new honeymoon.

"And people say I'm not sentimental!" she said.

He kissed her soft hair. "You're not —you're something better!"

THE ADVENTURES OF
AN UNCLE

THE ADVENTURES OF
AN UNCLE

"AND the dearest thing in the world, as you might say!" concluded Miss Gillatt, helping herself to a lettuce sandwich.

"I adore a gray-haired man who isn't really old, said Miss Wyckoff thoughtfully, "it looks so exciting and so—oh, it makes their eyes so—so—"

"Yes, indeed, and that's just the way Uncle Jimmie's eyes are! But he's old, Ursula; he's forty-two, you know. You can say anything to him, and that's such a comfort."

"Like a doctor," mused Ursula. "My sister married one, and I never had such fascinating conversations with anybody—"

Dodo dropped a leaf of berries and shook out her skirts, folding her hands primly and assuming a look of gleaming intelligence.

"The parlor: midnight: Ursula and her brother-in-law on a sofa!" she announced. Then very gushingly: " 'Oh, William, dear, how *wildly* interesting! And now tell me about measles; how soon do the symptoms appear? How does it differ from spinal meningitis? Could a parrot have it?' " With an air of heavy solemnity: " 'Your intelligent and stimulating questions, dear Ursula, delight me beyond words. As to the disease to which you refer—' "

Her pompous earnestness was unspeakably funny and their laughter drowned the rest. Ursula alone remained calm.

94

"You mistake the character of our conversations, my child," she remarked placidly. "They're quite different, I assure you."

They were taking supper on the back campus in a rural mood. Dodo, an awkward, big-boned creature, with a humorous homely face, sprawled across the roots of a tree, displaying large worn tan boots and a short skirt of ugly length. Ursula, in blue dotted piqué, with blue stockings, the latest fad in blue bandanna four-in-hands, and an immaculate white walking hat with a blue scarf, looked like a picture of the "well-dressed woman in the country." Miss Gillatt and Caroline, broad-shouldered, tanned, shirt-waisted and golf-booted, were of the type most popular with visiting parents. "A fine, all-round, well-developed, healthy, clever girl, sir! Look at those shoulders! I

95

tell you, education's a fine thing for girls nowadays!''

It was the last of May, and as the season was early, very hot. Commencement was not yet in the air, examinations were still distant, the spring was most enticing, and they loafed about and occupied themselves chiefly with being fond of the college. Nan had elaborated a theory that in case they should die prematurely they would undoubtedly regret having failed to utilize artistically the four Northampton spring terms that were theirs by right, so they avoided this sad possibility by driving, walking, and picnicking industriously.

To-day they were more silent than usual. Nan watched the clouds vaguely; Dodo was in one of her histrionic moods when only paraphrases of her friends indicated her power of speech; Ursula was in one of her rare fits of cynicism; and Caroline, who was quite accustomed to playing audience to the other three, waited for them comfortably and ate animal crackers meanwhile, a favorite article of diet with her.

"I think he's had experiences and things," Nan continued, aiming berries at Dodo's expectant mouth, "and you always feel he understands, you know, and—"

"Understands what?" interrupted Ursula, with the nearest approach to a snap that a person of almost perfect manners can be guilty of making. Nan stared sleepily at her.

"Why *you,* you know—women. He's the kind that calls you 'little girl'—"

"And a most disgusting kind, from my point of view—*n'est-ce-pas,* Dodo?" remarked Ursula, calmly.

"Nobody calls me that, honey, so I don't know. I'm not that kind, mesilf."

"Thank Heaven!"

"—and knows what you mean without your saying it," continued Nan, "and has that little jolly twinkle (if you'll sit more sideways, Caroline, my lamb, I can put my head in your lap), and is always ready for a spree and manages one so nicely! You miss all that up here, somehow—"

"Oh, dear! Now we've got to take her through it!" murmured Ursula. "Why didn't you say in the beginning, Nan, that you felt this way? When you get *ewig weibliche* you're always worse out here or in Paradise! Who is it? Don't say it's that idiotic youth that walked up the back of my gray crêpon!"

"If you mean Stanley Hewlitt, he's far from idiotic: he drew three honors and the Stafford prize essay. And if you *will* wear a train as long as you are—''

''There, there, don't scrap!'' interposed Caroline, the peacemaker. ''If Nan wants the little youths, let her have 'em—what's the odds, so long as she's happy? And she doesn't have 'em often. She's very reasonable.''

''Only in the spring—when they're *lightly turning,* I suppose,'' murmured Ursula.

The picture of Mr. Hewlitt lightly turning to anything—he was six feet two and very massive—affected the quartette similarly and simultaneously, and they burst into laughter.

''Just the same, Stan Hewlitt's a fine-looking man. I wouldn't have a man a scrap smaller. I detest little men: snappy tempers, and so suspicious. When I marry—''

"He must be enormous," interrupted Ursula.

"He must prefer hotels to housekeeping," said Caroline quickly.

"He must wear a long top-coat," added Dodo earnestly.

And then in a solemn chorus they intoned with a unanimity born of long practice:

"He must have three syllables in his name and never touch onions in any form!"

This ceremony over they looked at her politely.

"You were saying—" suggested Ursula.

"Oh, very well! If it amuses you to make such idiots of yourselves, keep it up, do! When you get in that state—"

"*We* aren't in any state that I know of," said Caroline placidly. "We—"

" 'Speaking of soup tureens, let's have some pie!' " interrupted Nan; "here comes the angel, now! Dear Uncle James, how-do-you-do? And kindly inform me how you got here."

Dear Uncle James removed his soft hat, displaying crisp silvery hair over a pair of young dark eyes, and sat down gracefully beside his niece.

"A charming young lady—a *very* charming young lady, dressed in pink with a kind of fringe-y trimming—most taking and dangly, I assure you—said that by going right ahead and looking for four girls eating to beat the band, I couldn't fail to find you. I see no band, but," with a comprehensive glance at the remains of the feast, "I judged that you have beaten it!"

"We have had a very pleasant luncheon," rejoined his niece, "but there is always room for one more, you know! Let me introduce my Uncle Jimmie Deane, Miss Bent, Miss Wyckoff, Miss Wilde. He is a very nice old party, I assure you all.''

As Dodo expressed it later, it was just as if he hadn't been there—they had so much fun. Dodo disliked men; she found them a great waste of time.

''But Mr. Deane hasn't any airs,'' she explained. Ursula laughed.

''You old silly, it's just because he has so *much* air that he's so nice,'' she said. ''And then, he's older, too. He hasn't got to be conscious all the time. It's boys you hate, Dody. You like the fathers, you know.''

''That's true,'' Dodo agreed. ''There's Mr. Gillatt and Mr. Bradford and your Dad—I love 'em all. ·But Mr. Deane, somehow, makes me think of a boy, too;

102

he isn't exactly like a father. There's a sort of difference—''

Ursula laughed aloud.

''I should say there was!'' she said. ''He's just Nan, grown up and turned into a man. I never knew where she got her ways—she's not a bit like her father, you know. Well, I suppose we sha'n't see much of her now. He's too fascinating to go shares in.''

And so for a while it seemed. Uncle Jimmie hung around the steps of the Main Building till Nan came out of chapel, learned her schedule for the day, and turned up at ten minutes past various hours with remarkable facility. They walked in Paradise and drove to Old Hadley and dined at queer places that Uncle Jimmie discovered. In the intervals he ''snooped about,'' as he said, and collected ''mental snapshots of the menagerie.'' It all interested him vastly. His descriptions of her mates were a never-ending joy to Nan and those favored few to whom she retailed them.

''Who is that tall, pompous person whose clothes match her hair and who feels the terrible responsibility of holding up the place, my sweet child? 'If I am taken, Heaven help poor Smith!' she shudders.''

''Oh, lovely! That's Esther Everetts. She's President of the Council.''

''She's really more like a parade than one person walking, isn't she? I always want to throw up my hat and cheer when she goes by—she takes quite an appreciable time to pass a given point, as it were!''

Coming out from a lecture she would be grabbed at the steps and begged to look

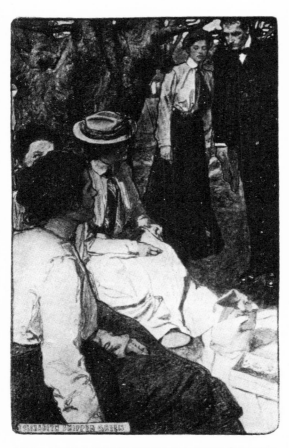

"'LET ME INTRODUCE MY UNCLE JIMMIE DEANE'"

at the fourth girl from the one in the queer-looking waist.

"Oh, there—you've missed her! Never mind. She's big—of a bigness I never saw, with dark red hair and a cream-colored skin—"

"That must be Frances B. Northrop."

"Oh, her name must be longer! And such a calm superiority, such a placidity, such a self-possession—"

"Oh, Evangeline! Evangeline it is, Uncle Jimmie. Do you think she's handsome?"

"Handsome? Of course—but no, she's not. And still—I don't know. Who is she? What does *she* do?"

"She just looks that way. Anybody else?"

"Yes, a little prize-fighter with twinkling little eyes and a little turn-up nose and her little fists in balls. She walks like a sailor on shore—and a whole basket of chips on her shoulder."

"That's Babe Stowe—Beecher Stowe, you know. She's sixteen. They put her off the freshman team because of her grade, and the freshmen were simply wild. But Miss Kassan said her game was too rough, anyway."

"I think I'd rather play on her side, myself."

Ursula and Dodo were elaborating, unknown to Nan, a most artistic *brochure* with burnt-leather covers and parchment leaves, each page bearing one of Ursula's inimitable caricatures of Uncle Jimmie's word portraits, with his remarks done in the exquisite Old English script that Dodo's big fingers could trace so rapidly and surely.

Esther, Evangeline, and the Babe, with a dozen others, were there: the poster

girl, in the long-waisted red golf jacket;
the artistic blonde with red-gold hair and
a Canton-blue blouse; the plump and jolly
president of the alphabetical religious or-
ganization—Uncle Jimmie called it the
Y. P. S. C. M. A. W. C. T. U.—who was
so preëminently and professionally
cheery and bright that one yearned to
throw a plate at her; the wide-eyed
genius, smiling fraternally at the big cast
of Shakespeare and murmuring,
"Hello!" to the head of the Literature
Department; the music student, with the
small waist and the high pompadour who
said: "I beg your pardon, but will you
please repeat the question?" till the class
giggled when her name was called: all
these adorned the leaves of Uncle
Jimmie's book.

It was to have been saved till the elastic
date of his departure, but it leaked out,

and Nan could not wait. So he saw it the moment it was done and pronounced it with a gratifyingly judicious air absolutely the cleverest thing he had ever seen. On the strength of it he gave a drive around the Notch and a seven-course dinner at Boyden's.

"Five is a nasty number, and six looks like a Sunday school picnic," Nan complained. "Somebody must cut the drive. I'd stay, but they wouldn't have it. So you must pick out the favored two, dear Uncle James."

This dear Uncle James flatly refused to do. "We can't spare one," he said, politely. "That heavenly Dodo—she must come or we'd be dull. I don't see what you'd do without Caroline to listen to you, Nan, do you? You can't talk to the horses. And—"

He paused. "Then you don't want Ursula?"

108

"Why, Nan, how ridiculous! Why on earth shouldn't I want Miss Wyckoff? You yourself suggested—"

"I suggested leaving somebody out, but I never imagined 'twould be Ursula. You· are the strangest man, Uncle Jimmie! Of all people, I should expect you to fall in love with Ursula—everybody does. And you haven't liked her from the first."

"What nonsense!"

"Not at all—you haven't. We've all noticed it. Only last night we were saying—"

"For Heaven's sake! Nan, have you suggested to Miss Wyckoff—"

"Oh, there, there! Calm yourself, dear. I haven't, of course. But why don't you like her? Don't you think she's clever?"

"Beyond a doubt."

"I know she isn't pretty, but she's so well-dressed and her figure is lovely, though she is so small—I thought you liked small women?"

"She's a very stylish girl."

"And she's older, too, and I thought you'd like that. I know we get awfully kiddish sometimes, but Ursula never does."

"Ah! little women are always dignified. Is she much older than the average?"

"She's a little over twenty-four. You see, she didn't intend to come to college, and she had finished at one of the big boarding-schools, and then suddenly decided to come."

"I see; it's your drive, my dear, and you will ask just whom *you* please. I only thought that Caroline seemed particularly your chum, and—"

"Oh, bless you, that's all right! She's assisting in Lab, now, anyway, and I don't believe she could come. So you'll have to put up with Ursula—you needn't sit with her—"

"My dear girl, you rave—are your chocolate peppermints out? Shall I get some more?"

He strolled off the piazza toward the village, and Nan proceeded to devote the hour before luncheon to the comparison of three psychology notebooks.

She had more company and showed the effect of it less than any of her friends. This may have been, as they said, because she was so clever; or as those obviously jealous and uninvited to assist at the various functions maintained, because her guests were so charming and so sociably inclined that Nan's friends were only too glad to repair with all the assistance in

111

their power the occasional educational breaches inevitably consequent to so much hospitality.

A rapid assimilation of Ursula's pointed flowing characters, Dodo's round business hand, and Caroline's jotted formulæ and diagrams brought her to luncheon time, and with a pleased consciousness of being the envy and admiration of a tableful of maidens whose uncles rarely came to visit them and never stayed, she sailed into the dining-room.

Here a series of unfortunate events occurred. They had baked beans for luncheon, which she detested; the lady-in-charge inadvertently addressed her as "Annie," which alone was enough to cast a gloom over her day; and a criticism of her interpretation of her Dramatics part conveyed by one of her friends added the last irritating touch. She stalked gloomily from the room at the conclusion of the meal and approached the waiting carriage with what was known to the house as her Edwin Booth air. Dodo and Uncle Jimmie, utterly unconscious of the occasion for such a change of manner, tried in vain to win her back to ordinary terms of association. She derived great satisfaction from including them all in the condemnation, and with a vague feeling that it was no more than he deserved, she motioned Dodo to share the back seat of the carriage with her, leaving Ursula to mount beside the driver.

Remembering that he had not, in spite of his denials of any such discrimination, talked much with Ursula, she rather counted on Uncle Jimmie's maintaining a somewhat embarrassing silence, leaving Ursula to entertain him; but far from justifying these sombre apprehensions, Uncle Jimmie seemed to have nerved himself to make the best of a bad bargain —his partiality for Dodo was well known —and positively outdid himself in charm and rattling gayety. At first he tried to draw Nan into it, as Dodo sat directly behind him, but his niece, though excessively polite, failed to take up his points and throw them back with her ordinary practiced ease, and at last, with an almost perceptible shrug, Uncle Jimmie gave up the attempt and devoted himself entirely to Ursula, who was looking her best in lavender and white, with a big white hat and small rosettes of lavender ribbon here and there.

His gallantry was highly successful. Ursula, who had hitherto confined her admiration of Uncle Jimmie's wit and wisdom to evening talks with Dodo, now displayed it openly, and when Ursula reached the intelligently appreciative point one was apt to discover that her eyes were fine. As Nan would not talk, and Dodo was a little tired—she made up for Nan's dissipations by getting up at unchristian hours in the morning to study —they depended on bits of the front seat conversation to break the silence of the rear. One of these bits, a quick exclamation of Ursula's, caught Nan's attention.

"Oh, Mr. Deane, that's just it! That's just what I've always thought since I came here. But how did you see it so clearly? You must be more—"

She broke off abruptly.

"More serious than you thought?" continued Uncle Jimmie placidly. "Well, perhaps I am, you know. It's a great mistake, Miss Wyckoff, to imagine that

115

because a man makes fun of the great changes that women are going through nowadays he doesn't really feel terribly interested. Of course, *young* men—'' he paused. Nan knew by the tone that he was embarked on one of his half-droll, half-serious speculations, and it was on such occasions that the mixture of philosophy, intimacy, and flattering frankness to which he treated his listener made Uncle Jimmie peculiarly fascinating. Nan leaned forward: her sulkiness vanished as quickly as it had come.

''Oh, talk louder, you people!'' she cried, eagerly. ''We can't hear and we're *so* interested!''

Uncle Jimmie turned, and with the most delicious and apparently unconscious imitation of his niece's Vere-de-Vere accent replied with elaborate regret.

''So sorry! But I can't well turn

116

because of the horses. I'm really extremely sorry!''

Dodo chuckled as his back appeared again; and the increased pace of the team, whereat the carriage rattled, rendered the voices ahead little more than a murmur.

Nan had the grace to smile, and as Dodo was tactful and talked from time to time, she slowly recovered her ordinary manner. But Uncle Jimmie was lost to her. Dodo and he exchanged a word now and then, but Nan knew that she was being punished and tried to take it as gracefully as might be.

At the dinner which followed nobody knew which to admire the more, Uncle Jimmie or Ursula. Usually a little reserved, she came out wonderfully when she was deeply interested, and now that she really knew Uncle Jimmie she was interested beyond a doubt. It was she, not Nan, who took up his most character- istic sallies, and it was soon apparent that for conversation they might depend upon these two. It seemed as if Uncle Jimmie wanted to make up for his previous indif- ference by the noticeable attention he paid her, and Ursula's ease under the combined scrutiny of her new and old friends recalled to them, as something occasionally did, her greater social ex- perience and a training more varied than their own.

At the appearance of the coffee a sud- den little gravity fell over them all.

"This is because," Ursula explained with a bright smile at Uncle Jimmie, "we are realizing that regal as all this is, we don't get the thrill that we got when we sat up after ten, freshman year, to make fudge in a chafing-dish. It's ridiculous,

118

but I think I was more scared then than I ever was in my life—you remember, Nan?''

"I do, indeed. We were at Miss Whipple's, freshman year, Uncle Jimmie, and she was so strict! I thought I should be flayed alive if she caught me. It was such fun!''

"Actually, I had such lumps in my throat, I couldn't swallow my fudge!'' continued Ursula. "I quaked in every limb. Now I don't want to sit up to make it. If I did I shouldn't be afraid, anyhow. This is so conventional, so suitable, so approved of by every one. Why, even Mrs. Austin smiled on me when I told her, and said what a pleasant time we were having, and that she thought it did everybody good to eat a meal occasionally in a different place! Wasn't that terribly reasonable? There isn't any really sinful thing to do—there are no rules that it would be only sensible to break. I wish there were. It's rules that make such charming sins!''

"And all the commandments put premiums on vice!'' added Uncle Jimmie sympathetically. "Poor girls! Where are the sins of yesteryear? Isn't there anything we could do?''

"Nothing at all,'' returned Ursula decidedly. "Dodo and I have lain awake nights thinking over every possible thing. Once we even went to Springfield and went to the theatre and stayed over night at a hotel, but—''

"It wasn't all their fancy painted,'' said Nan, with a grin. "At dinner Ursula saw a man that she knew, and coming back after the play she saw him, too, and she thought he looked surprised and she was overcome with remorse—''

"'IF IT IS A QUESTION OF YOUTH, MR. DEANE, WHY,
DRINK TO US ONLY WITH THINE EYES'"

"Not at all. I merely felt—"

"You felt dreadfully, Ursula," Dodo interrupted, "and you talked all night about what he probably thought."

"Dear me," observed Uncle Jimmie, "that young man had a great deal on his shoulders."

"Oh, he wasn't a young man," explained Nan. "Ursula scorns them. About forty, she says. That's why—" with an audacious wink at Uncle Jimmie, recalling his brief replies to her panegyrics on Ursula's charms—"that's why she likes you!"

Ursula looked as nearly embarrassed as anybody ever saw her, and Uncle Jimmie, with the courteous ease that distinguished him in any such situation, raised his coffee-cup.

"In that case, here's to plenty of rules and a fascinating crime attached to every

121

one!'' he exclaimed. ''If any one so aged as myself may presume to share the toast,'' he added. ''Crabbed age and youth, you know—''

Ursula shot a queer glance at Nan.

''Oh, youth!'' she said lightly. ''If it is a question of youth, Mr. Deane, why, drink to us only with thine eyes!''

This felicitous appreciation of the discrepancy between Uncle Jimmie's eyes and hair evoked actual applause, and, as Nan admitted, was well worth the look he gave her for it.

The day after the dinner Uncle Jimmie was called to New York, but he left solemn promises for all Commencement week, and the flowers and candy that filled the hall table after his departure softened the blow materially. Nan regretted a little that he had not been better able to keep up his later attitude toward

122

Ursula in his parting presents. While Dodo was overwhelmed by the appearance of some beautiful orchids—she had characteristically complained that she rarely got flowers, and had never, like a real lady, drawn any orchids from her admirers—and Nan reveled in an immense bunch of the English violets Uncle Jimmie never failed to get for her in all seasons, and Caroline's American Beauties scented her hall for days, Ursula was obliged to content herself with pansies: an enormous box of them, to be sure, and each one richly colored, but at best not to be compared with the other tributes.

"That's just like a man, but not like Uncle Jimmie," Nan confided to Caroline. "Now what is it to her that pansies happen to be his favorite flower? They're not hers. Usually Uncle Jimmie's very canny about his presents—he gives you

123

what *you* want: he's not like other relatives—but I suppose his invention gave out. After orchids and violets and American Beauties there's really nothing left."

They had all realized that Commencement week could not be in any sense a repetition of Uncle Jimmie's visit. But they had not allowed for the utter difference. The group, in fact, was very much broken up.

Dodo's father was a shy man and wanted to be alone with her; Caroline's family had never been in the town and had to be escorted everywhere; and Nan's relatives, from very acquaintance with persons and places, somehow demanded more attention than as if they had had only Nan to talk to. That, at least, was her explanation of why her time was almost completely taken up.

124

THE ADVENTURES OF AN UNCLE

Ursula's father and mother and little sister came for one day only, however, and as she had no other guests she was mistress of her time to an unusual extent. This Nan realized—as indeed did all her friends—and besought her to "go and play with my loved ones! I know Uncle Jimmie is bored to death—I'm so disappointed not to see more of him—I don't get a minute to myself! It's horrid not to see you girls at all, just horrid! Do be nice to him, Ursula: you're about the only free person he knows!"

"But perhaps he'd rather—"

"Oh, dear, no! He sees enough of the rest of them. This isn't Thanksgiving, you know, and family reunions at Commencement are ghastly, I think."

The week was over at last, and the relatives drifted away and the lanterns were pulled down, and the road to the opera house was no longer filled with people in veils and party cloaks. Gardeners, carpenters, and cleaning-women lorded it everywhere, and the few college people that stayed over for any reason loved each other dearly, they were so rare.

The four, with two others, were going directly to Nan's summer home in Sconset, and were as tired and cross and nervous as important seniors ought to be.

"I know I'm as ugly as sin, and I'm better off alone," Nan said frankly, and they all agreed to pack by themselves.

So when Dodo came into the single room that Nan had lived in three years, and sat on the bed very much in the way, glowering at nothing, Nan, worn out in the effort to pack two party gowns, a tennis racquet and a large bath sponge

126

into an already overflowing tray, was divided between rage at the interruption and amazement at Dodo's very unusual attitude.

"For Heaven's sake, Theodora Margaret Bent, say something, or get out!" she cried at last. "What *is* the matter with you? You can't live here always, can you? There, you've been sitting on my bath-wrapper all the time! Why didn't you say so?"

Dodo handed her the wrapper with no answer but a sigh.

"Are you sick?" Nan demanded, less ungraciously. "Is anything wrong?"

"I should say there— No, of course not. There's nothing wrong. But you'll be very much surprised. I have to tell you, because otherwise Ursula won't come—"

"Now what nonsense is this? Why

127

won't she come? If it's because of poor Uncle Jimmie, I must say Ursula's very childish. She needn't see him much, anyhow. There's no earthly reason why they shouldn't like each other. I think it's the strangest thing—"

"But you don't understand, I say! She *does* like him!"

"Well, then, what's the row?" demanded Nan, sharply.

"And—and he likes her!" was the halting response.

Dodo's awkward, constrained manner struck deeper than her words. Nan sat down abruptly.

"What do you mean?" she said shortly.

"They are—they are in love with each other!" Dodo blurted out, defiantly.

Nan sat perfectly still, and the little clock sounded too loud for belief for a

128

"'FOR HEAVEN'S SAKE, THEODORA MARGARET
BENT, **SAY** SOMETHING, OR GET OUT !'"

few seconds.   Presently she began to talk
in a dazed way.

"Why—why, he doesn't like—she
never said—I don't believe it! Who
said so?"

"Ursula told me herself," was the
reply.

Nan stared at her. "When did she
say that?"

"Last night. She knew how you'd
feel. She's all cut up about it, but she
says it's all your fault."

"My fault?"

"Yes. When she saw him the very
first time she thought he was the nicest
man she ever saw. And he thought she
was, too—I don't mean the nicest man,
of course. And he was afraid he'd be—
afraid he'd—he didn't wish to, you know,
because she was too young, he thought,
and so he tried not to think about it. And

she did, too—she thought of course he'd never care for her. Then you acted so that day we went to drive, and they were so disgusted with you they just let go. That began it. He thought she was just clever and not anything else, and that's what she thought about him, and that day they found out that there was more to them—each other, I mean—and even then he was going away, and you told him that evening that she liked older men, and it irritated her and she said that thing about his eyes, and then they knew it was so—''

"How do *you* know what he thought all the time?"

"He told Ursula," said Dodo simply. Nan moved impatiently.

"Go on," she said.

"Then he sent her a letter in those flowers, and said that of course he was too old and it was too much to ask—and she says she wouldn't marry anybody a week younger—and at Commencement you kept teasing her to entertain him, and she said she felt like such a sneak, because she wanted to, and he took her out in a canoe and then she said she did, and—''

''She *did?*''

''Why, yes. Liked him, you know. And she says that not unless you forgive her and are willing. She knows how fond you are of him. She knew how you'd feel.''

''We were going to be together—I was going to be his housekeeper—Oh, dear, dear, dear!''

Nan burst into nervous tears and the bed shook.

Dodo patted her head, gulping occasionally herself.

131

"It's all so different now," she said jerkily; "it seems as if college were all over now. I had an idea we'd just keep on, somehow, the same way. Of course I was a fool. But she's awfully fond of him, Nan."

There was no answer.

"And you ought to remember, Nan, that you egged them on, really."

Nan's sobs shaded off into hysterical giggles.

"Did you ever know anything so funny?" she gasped. "*I* kept telling him how nice she was! *I* told him she was older. *I* told him everything! Did you ever know such a fool? And we never knew, we never suspected! How stupid we were!"

Dodo shook her head.

"*I* don't know how it's done," she said, scornfully. "I supposed they sighed and languished, and all that, when they were that way. Caroline never knew, either. But—but isn't it unusually quick?" she asked, doubtfully.

Nan wiped her eyes and straightened her hair.

"They are neither of them what you'd call slow," she answered calmly. "I'm going in to see her. I'd rather she'd have him than anybody else, for that matter. And I'll tell you this, Dodo, that when *you* do it I'd prefer that you'd let me know when I begin to make a complete idiot of myself."

Dodo sniffed.

"Oh, me!" she said, expressively.

"I know where they'll go—to Algiers!" Nan burst out. "He was going to take me. And Ursula gets dreadfully seasick."

She reached the door.

133

"If I happen to say that I knew it all the time, or anything like that, you're to keep still," she remarked.

With her hand on the door-knob she paused again.

"All is not lost!" she cried. "I can't very well say Aunt Ursula, and I shall call him Jimmie! I've always wanted to!"

Ursula met her in the hall and Dodo heard them talking excitedly and both at once.

"Put it on! Put it on, I tell you!"

Nan's voice reached her.

"The idea! Of course I am! You were made for each other. Wait till he comes, and see me do the 'bless-you-my-children' act."

Her voice grew fainter down the hall. "Oh, see the pansies!" Dodo just heard. "What an extravagant Jimmie!"

134

THE ADVENTURES OF AN UNCLE

Dodo took up Nan's packing and completed the tray. As she sat on the lid, jouncing up and down in a businesslike way, with a towel in her hand for a handkerchief—Ursula seemed so far away from them, suddenly—she sighed.

"I suppose they'll all come to it sooner or later!" she murmured, "all!"

THE POINT OF VIEW

THE POINT OF VIEW

BEING SIX BIRTHDAY LETTERS FROM HOME
TO MARY, A POPULAR AND PROMINENT
JUNIOR AT COLLEGE

I

MY DEAR MARY:—I am sending you by this mail, by way of birthday remembrance, a copy of my last book, *Our Bodies and the Care of Them.* I do not consider it by any means original, but twenty years spent in the practice of medicine have convinced me that the ignorance and carelessness of young people at an age when they should be storing up health and vitality are responsible for most of the sickness and suffering of the world.

139

HER FIANCÉ

I was called in lately to see Ethel Hayward, your friend and schoolmate, and found her utterly exhausted as a result of "too much fun," as she puts it. I was glad that you had chosen another career. But even at college I suppose there may be a slight temptation in that direction. I never found it myself while working for my diploma, but my temperament is more like your mother's, and you resemble your father. A little relaxation is necessary to health, but a strong young woman, with no personal responsibility and such opportunities as you have for extending her knowledge, should have little time for idling. With eight hours for work, nine for sleep (your father's family is a nervous one), three for meals, two for exercise in the open air, and two for your recreation, you should be abundantly able to live a healthful and at the same time a studious life. Regularity, good food, exercise: with these you will not need to consult me. Read especially in the book chapter eleven on "Exercise for the Student."

With so much leisure time as you must have (no dressmaking or household duties), why do you not take up a good course in chemistry? Greek and Latin and French are all very well, but in this day and generation the unscientific are the truly uneducated. I hope you will consider this.

With affectionate wishes,

AUNT MARGARET.

II

DEAR MAY:—I suppose by this time you have received the box I sent you—I haven't had a moment to write. It is all very well to say Lent, but the dancing

141

classes—and they meet here this season —and Kitty's sewing afternoons—you know they do that so much in Boston, and we thought we'd try it here—and the duplicate whist, and the D. A. R. always doing something, it's really no rest at all.

The bolero jacket I hope you'll like— Mrs. Pendleton got it through the custom-house with her own things. The medallion belts are very much worn over there, she says, so I tucked one in.

I do hope you're keeping up your French and your dancing. Of course you'd get little if any chance to dance— Kitty says it isn't taught at Smith. I must say I think it is odd—but can't you join a class in Boston? You're near there, I know. And don't, my dear child, don't, I beg of you, take any study where you dissect anything. It makes a

142

girl so unattractive. Mr. Stevens said yesterday that he was really afraid to visit at the Hendersons'—you know they say Lilly dissected a cat at some laboratory. You see how *he* felt.

Of course you have a great deal of time if you've dropped your music and riding. I hope you continue to call on the Northrops and the Miss Underhills, and don't forget those families in Springfield I gave you cards to. You can't have too many desirable acquaintances. Do be careful to be nice to Mrs. Stuyver's niece. She's only been there this year—she went last fall—and I told Mrs. Stuyver that you would call on her frequently and make it pleasant for her. Have her in that society you said was so desirable—was it the "Alpha"? I assured Mrs. Stuyver that you would invite her into it immediately. Of course any

143

such little attention will be appreciated, and the Stuyvers are such a fine family.

I hope your box from home will be enjoyed—Louise told me about the nut-cake. But don't over-eat—you know your mother's people have simply no digestion at all, and you don't want to be as sallow as your aunt Margaret.

With love from Kitty,

AUNT GRACE.

III

DEAR MAMIE:— I told Ethel yesterday to mail you a copy of Dr. Cope's *Lenten Thoughts* from me, and to-day I sent your mother two silver tablespoons; your dozen of forks was completed at Christmas, if I remember rightly. Please pardon Ethel's writing "to my grand-child" instead of "to my godchild." I did not want to waste the book, however.

144

THE POINT OF VIEW

I hope you are constantly bearing in
mind, my dear girl, that it is not what you
know, but what you *believe,* that is going
to count in this world and the world to
come. Mere book learning is a poor
thing, indeed, unless it strengthens our
faith. And too often it does not do this
—we have terrible examples of it. I
hope that you do not allow your mind
to be occupied by your studies to the
extent that you forget the far more important hours of meditation and religious and charitable work. Dr. Cope
spoke so beautifully about that last Sunday.

I never begin Lent without a new
thankfulness for this sweet season of
rest. To drop all our cares and troubles,
to let the world and its rushing turmoil
go by and sit quietly with our thoughts,
is a very wholesome experience for us, in

these busy, feverish times, and you find it so, I am sure.

You are so fortunate in having Mr. Morton for your rector. From what I know of him he would be certain to help you a great deal. Of course you take advantage of the daily services. Dr. Cope thinks their value simply inestimable. A half-hour a day is little to give.

You have, of course, much unoccupied time; my only criticism of the life you are leading is its freedom from all outside responsibility. But it has its advantages in Lent. Your studies over for the day, why not make out a programme for the rest of the time? I have found that an hour for service, an hour for quiet reading (Ethel and I are going through Bishop Brooks's sermons), and my guild sewing in the evening make a beautiful close to the day.

THE POINT OF VIEW

I have Ethel make her bed, and, indeed, spare the maid the care of her room during Lent, and we have the simplest desserts. Could you not do something like that? Then, perhaps, others would follow your example.

And try to withdraw yourself. There is too much going and coming in life nowadays, though a studious young girl probably sees little of that. But so far as you can, quietly refrain from making new friends, however innocent and desirable. I know that many people, your aunt Mrs. Eustace, for example, think me an extremist, but better far to err on the side of religion (if that were possible!) than on the side of *social success!*

Your loving godmother,

MARY SEAMAN.

HER FIANCÉ

IV

My Dear Molly:—To-morrow, if I remember rightly, is your birthday. I
have just forwarded a little remembrance to Lillian Henderson: and that
put me in mind that your birthdays were
very close together. I never forget my
old Homer class, you see! You were the
first girls to fit for college from Miss
Taylor's, and I assure you that your
influence is felt in the school yet. I do
not need to ask if you are holding up
our standard! In the hands of all of
you girls lies the future reputation for
scholarly work of this generation of
women, you know. It will not be the
girls who went to dances nor the girls
who made their fame (?) at golf, but the
girls who showed their ability to meet
with men on their own ground, and

prove their equality, nay, their essential
superiority, that will lift this century
higher. Three of my girls go up to
Smith next September; they will not
disgrace the school, for they think nothing of taking the Harvard entrance
examination papers as weekly tests. I
look forward to the time when the Harvard papers will be no better test than
those of any woman's college. From all
I can hear, there will soon be entrance
requirements in football. At least such
folly is spared you girls.

While I approve heartily of all reasonable gymnastic exercise, I regret very
much the tone of exaggerated deference
to athletic honors that seems to be creep-
ing in even among women. The girls
are overdoing golf and fencing, in my
opinion, as Miss Taylor understands
perfectly. From a hint dropped by

149

HER FIANCÉ

Lillian I gathered that this spirit was in evidence to a certain extent at Smith.

I hope, dear Molly, that you will not let your natural quickness and interest in new things distract you from your chief interest just now—your scholarly rank, which ought to be high. There in that delightful academic atmosphere, with hundreds of students all working with you, with the impetus of a skilled body of instructors, with libraries at your hand, surely you have no opportunity nor desire to waste any of that precious time in childish games and faddish sports. I remember my own three years at Mount Holyoke; I could never find hours enough in the day.

Take a walk before supper, and if you need it, a little work with the dumbbells before retiring, but these ten-mile tramps can only tire the body to exhaustion.

Now, while you have such leisure as you will probably never know again, for no teacher, no housekeeper and mother, no breadwinner in any field, can hope for it, do the little extra things that make for real scholarship.

Do not be carried away by this wave of scientific fascination that is turning even our girls away from literature and the classics to chemistry and physics. Latin·and Greek are to-day as they were yesterday, and will be to-morrow, the touchstone for the cultured man or woman. Instead of reading some novel or doing fancy-work when you get together with your friends, try the last twelve books of the Odyssey, or some Ovid; they make delightful reading. Try it for an hour, even a half-hour a day,

151

and note the result. It will help your class-work wonderfully.

I hope you will like the photograph of the Coliseum; I sent the Parthenon to Lillian.

Don't forget that I want to see you all M. A.'s some fine day!

Your friend and old teacher,

SUSAN C. McVEIGH.

v

DEAR OLD MOLLYWOG:—How's twenty-one? Feel big, I suppose. We sent the box yesterday, and father put in the soda-mints in the bottom. If the nut-cake doesn't suit, send it back; it does all right for me!

Father says we don't hear from you enough, so hurry up and let us know about the box. Mrs. Seaman's spoons turned up and mother's put them in the safe. I think she's an old—well, I won't say so, but I think so. She blew mother up because we had meat for luncheon. The idea! I hope, for goodness' sake, you won't take after her, if you *are* named after her! Don't you waste your good time reading sermons, will you? Don't you get out of practice, because there's a Miss Spooner here that puts up a mighty good game, she drives to beat the band. She goes over the links once a day, rain or shine.

Now take an hour, say from three to four every day, *and do it.* Will you? You can, just as well as not. What have you got to do? I have to water all the flowers and see to the table flowers every day, and keep the laundry-book, besides my practicing. And you won't even write every Sunday. You ought to be ashamed.

HER FIANCÉ

Father says to make a point of learning Robert's Rules of Orders, whatever they are, and conduct a meeting intelligently. Make up a club of some sort, he says, and practice once a week or so. He says better belong to that one good solid club and get the good out of it, than waste your strength on those others where you just eat things, as far as we can see. So there's that and the golf, and don't forget your basket-ball, if you *are* a junior! They play here now, you know, and I want you to surprise them Easter vacation. So practice twice a week, anyhow, won't you? Practice with the freshmen, the way Miss Harriet does. Give her my love and keep a lot for yourself. I hope you like the nut-cake. From your own

Lou.

THE POINT OF VIEW

VI

MA CHÈRE MARIE:—To think that we are twenty-one! Though really I don't feel so—I feel just like the younger girls. Were you surprised when you saw the pillow? We thought you'd be. We were all taken in shirt-waists to look all alike—I think they transferred beautifully. Elsie wanted the autographs in different colors, but I *insisted* on the gold thread! I hope you will tumble to the idea, Mlle. Marie—we shall be *terribly bored* if you don't. We said we'd try to keep "the crowd" together, but some of us are drifting off a little tiny bit, *n'est ce pas?* I know you're having a dindy time there, but, after all, the "school crowd" is the first crowd, isn't it? Since I've heard so much about it I've been a little bit sorry papa thought I'd better

155

not, but all the same there are a *few*
things you don't have—the opera, for
instance. My dear, you should have
heard de Reszke! He was *absolutely
divine!* Fan and I burst our gloves at
Faust. You won't mind, *chérie,* if I
speak very *frankly* and beg you not to be
too—well, too "managing" when you
come in the spring? You know since
Lillian gave up and came back we've
had *all we could do* to squelch her, or we
should have been absolutely *sat on* all the
time! I suppose being president of her
class freshman year upset her, but it
does seem *absurd* that nobody can speak
without Lil jumping on them for "par-
liamentary law." When we were decid-
ing about Miss Taylor's tea for the
alumnæ, every time anybody *suggested*
anything, Lil pounded on the table and
kept saying we were *"out of order."* The

girls were terribly bored. Of course we haven't been to college, but we aren't *perfect* fools, you know. We know our own business, I should hope! So don't, for heaven's sake, *chérie,* learn those awful things that *nobody* cares about. I think it must be terribly nice to belong to those nice little societies Lil told about! I should get in as many as I could—she says that's the way to know the girls.

Now we don't want to be cross, but Fan hasn't had a letter for a month, and I haven't heard for *two weeks*. It isn't as if you lived in the city and had church work and dancing classes and all that. Way off there I should think you would *want* to write! There are just six of us altogether, you see, and why couldn't you write *one* of us every day? Then that would give you Sunday for your family —Lil says they all do that Sundays.

157

HER FIANCÉ

Why not do it in the evenings—there's nothing else to do, is there? Lil says there aren't any good plays except once an *age,* and, of course, you can't study *all* the time!

Has Fan said anything to you about anything? My dear, it's a *dead certainty.* I suppose you know who it is? I'm simply *wild* about it—I don't approve of it at all. But they say the family do. Still, it's not announced. I promised not to speak of it, but I suppose she's told *you.* Perhaps you'd better not mention it, though, when you write. And remember to do *one a day*—that's not much.

With *heaps* of love from

ETHEL.

THE POINT OF VIEW

PART II

BEING SEVEN BIRTHDAY NOTES FROM COL-
LEGE TO THE SAME

I

DEAR MISS MATTHEWS:—Will you
please direct and sign these Alpha invitations so they can go on the bulletin-
board to-morrow before chapel? Miss
Kinsman is very anxious to make the
invitations very personal, and get all our
Faculty, if possible. She said you knew
which they were and would see to it.

Very sincerely yours,

E. B. HOUGHTON,

(*Tuesday.*)   *Secretary.*

II

MOLLY DEAR:—I trust you don't forget
we said we would sing in the choir

Wednesdays? Esther wants us to come a little early to rehearse; you know Mr. Morton said he hoped there'd be more system this year.

Hastily,

J. S. C.

III

I know you will look in the glass, so I stick this here. William is going to have a written lesson—old snide! The whole Napoleon business, Russia and all. Cut French lit. and come up to 44. Isn't it vile? BAB.

IV

MY DEAR MISS MATTHEWS:—You have been selected as one of the most satisfactory members of the psychology class to be one of the "charter members" of the new psychology club. Please meet me in room 8 to-morrow (Wednesday),

160

to discuss in detail the arrangements for our first meeting. The hour is three o'clock promptly, as there is much to do, and we are late in beginning.

Yours truly,

JOHN B. TRAVIS.

v

DEAR MATTIE:—Mr. Henry has suddenly appeared and wants very much to see you. The doctor won't let me out, so we've had to fix it up with Bab and Julia for this morning, and I told him you'd take a walk or something from four to six. Now don't make any other plans, or else break 'em if you have, for I simply can't plan any further. He'll call for you. He's really very anxious to see you—probably a bid for something.

As ever,

ELSIE.

HER FIANCÉ

MY DEAR MISS MATTHEWS:—I regret
that I have been obliged to mark your
Hamlet paper very low. It shows every
sign of hurried, ill-considered writing,
which is a pity, for your ability is above
the average and your class-work satisfactory. I know for your own sake you
will change this condition of affairs as
soon as possible. If you will come to my
room any time between four and six this
afternoon I will go over it with you.

Sincerely yours,

LOUISE L. HITCHCOCK.

VII

DEAR SAINT MATTHEW:—Here are
twenty-one roses for twenty-one years,
and may you live long and prosper! Of
course I'll come to-night, and don't you
want some plates? I'll come at six and

help you get ready. Be sure and get dressed before that, as I want you to have a nice long chat with Edith Willard —she's perfectly fascinating. Do you want my knives? They're in the lower part of the wash-stand under the tin pans—you'll have to clean them. Don't upset those blue prints. I shall be in lab. all the afternoon. Where have you been all the morning? I've been in three times.   Until to-night,

                                        ALICE.

_____

PART III

BEING MARY'S BIRTHDAY SCHEDULE

———

8 to chapel; room ready for sweeping and ten pages German.

9-10—English lit.

10-11—German.

11-12—Read seventy pages history.

163

12-1—History.

1-1.30—Lunch.

1.30-2—House play committee.

2-3—Rehearse play.

3-3.30—Mandolin club (get a room).

3.30-4—Take golf dues from new members, old gym.

4-5—Walk with Helen (leave word in case H. L. B. comes).

5-5.30—Alpha committee (Lawrence House).

5.30-6—House meeting.

6-7—Dress and write Mrs. Seaman.

7-9—Spread (candles, rose-bowl, fifteen glasses, Alice's plates, knives?).

9-9.30—Bath.

9.30-10—Get lab. notes for quiz from Jess.

10—Write themes.

Query: Where was Mary's leisure time?

164